W9-AUD-996

KIWI
CANNOT REACH!

**WRITTEN AND ILLUSTRATED
BY JASON THARP**

Ready-to-Read

Simon Spotlight
New York London Toronto Sydney New Delhi

To all the Kiwis out there,
keep reaching for those dreams!
I believe in you.

SIMON SPOTLIGHT
An imprint of Simon & Schuster Children's Publishing Division
1230 Avenue of the Americas, New York, New York 10020
This Simon Spotlight edition May 2019
Copyright © 2019 by Jason Tharp
SIMON SPOTLIGHT, READY-TO-READ, and colophon are registered trademarks of Simon & Schuster, Inc.
For information about special discounts for bulk purchases, please contact Simon & Schuster Special Sales at
1-866-506-1949 or business@simonandschuster.com.
Manufactured in the United States of America 0319 LAK
10 9 8 7 6 5 4 3 2 1
Library of Congress Cataloging-in-Publication Data
Names: Tharp, Jason, author, illustrator.
Title: Kiwi cannot reach! / written and illustrated by Jason Tharp.
Description: New York : Simon Spotlight, 2019. | Series: Ready-to-read |
Summary: "Kiwi sees a rope. He wants to pull it, but he cannot reach! What will happen next? Beginning
readers can help Kiwi by turning the pages, shaking the book, and more in this interactive story"—Provided
by publisher.
Identifiers: LCCN 2019005404 | ISBN 9781534425118 (pbk) |
ISBN 9781534425125 (hc) | ISBN 9781534425132 (eBook)
Subjects: | CYAC: Determination (Personality trait)—Fiction. | Kiwis—Fiction. | Humorous stories. | BISAC:
JUVENILE FICTION / Readers / Beginner. | JUVENILE FICTION / Humorous Stories. | JUVENILE
FICTION / Animals / Birds.
Classification: LCC PZ7.1.T4473 Kiw 2019 | DDC [E]—dc23
LC record available at https://lccn.loc.gov/2019005404

Maybe I can pull it
if I jump really high.

You will?
Great! I have a plan.
All you have to do is push
this launch button.

Can you help me get down?
Try shaking the book up and down.

It worked!
Thank you for
shaking the book.

Do not worry.
I am not giving up
on that rope.
I bet this cannon
will do the trick!

On the count of three,
flip the switch.
One, two, three . . .

flip the
switch!

SWITCH

Uh-oh.

You blew a great bubble! I am flying!

Maybe it is time to give up.
At least I found this log to sit on.

Hooray!
I am pulling the rope!
I am so glad we tried
one more time.

We did it!